MARK TWAIN

IN OUTER

SPACE

By M.V. Montgomery

Mark Twain In Outer Space
Copyright © 2014 MV Montgomery

ISBN-13: 978-0615911960

First Serialized in Cowboy Poetry Press
Dime Novel Cover design © 2014 Red
Dashboard LLC

Published by Red Dashboard LLC
Publishing, Princeton NJ 08540
www.reddashboard.com

To My Literary Sister, Katie

MARK TWAIN IN OUTER SPACE

i. I arrive on the planet surface—am immediately disappointed—my battle against gravity—a digression concerning the naming of constellations

By the look of things, I had arrived too late for the planet's funeral. The soil had already been cremated, and set back on the geological shelf. I was disconsolate. I had hoped for a better vacation spot, nothing fancy mind you, just a garden to stroll around in, with a swimming pool, and some interesting animals to name. And—if it wasn't too much to ask—maybe a lonely siren, and a reasonably priced saloon.

Now I realized, sadly, that I had been done in by my own greed. For, gentle reader, the planet had hung for me like an apple for me in its distant, tantalizing orbit. And I had coveted it—coveted it over a span most humans can only dream of sinning across.

My coming had created quite a stir of things. For the longest time, I could see nothing but the dust clouds that had heralded my arrival. As for myself, I soon discovered I would have no more trouble with gravity on this planet, than I did on Earth. This was disheartening also. Because even if I couldn't have my garden, I might have been able to comfort myself by turning the planet into my wild gymnasium and soaring about it in fifty- and hundred-foot leaps. For fun, I could have lifted my ship over my head, tossed it hand to hand, or bounced it up and down like a child's ball—I could. Or perhaps I might have played the evil alien from outer space and stomped out a few Lilliputian villages for my own amusement. I choked to think how I had been cheated out of doing all the wonderful things my imagination conjured up for me.

In vain, I tried to stride across the planet's surface like a colossus, succeeding only in wrenching my legs. In vain, I leapt around, flapped my hopeful arms, and thought lofty thoughts, but did not find myself elevated in any way.

I blush to think of the spectacle I must have made of myself, performing all of these actions in ridiculous slow-motion. I can only find consolation in speculating that any intelligent being watching might not have possessed arms or legs, to know how better acquainted with mine I ought to have been. Or if he had, perhaps he would have taken some pity on me and offered his assistance—as I was apparently in considerable distress, having forgotten my limitations as a featherless biped.

It was a bad poet's sun: the color of a five-ball. So little out of the ordinary, that I set it down here for the scientific rather than the literary record. To compose a panegyric upon it would be like sticking a peruke on the town drunk and declaring him a district judge.

I observed, after all the destruction and turmoil that I could modestly attribute to my landing had subsided, that a steady sirocco was blowing. It might become significant to note here that I was struck by the impression that this was just the sort of breeze to have blowing on your side if you were carrying on an argument with your neighbor across the street.

I also thought I might have caught sight in the distance of a small shape rolling and bouncing by. But at the time, I dismissed this evidence of my eyes. I was feeling tired and somewhat dizzy from my recent attempts at levitation, which had re-taught me the old lesson that my humanity was a burden I must carry.

I looked again, but all I could see for miles around was the ashen sand—well, and a couple of cacti. But there was no sign of life that I could see.

I considered an immediate return to the ship, where I could read all about hacking through tropical jungles or trudging across desolate plains without having to experience such pleasures firsthand: for such is the wonder of the novel. But in my heart, I knew that once back in space, I would only fidget and toss my books aside, then pace up and down in front of the viewer screen, upon which each star would take on different personalities as my cabin fever set in—appearing, at first, as a novelty—then as a breathtaking firework—then as a beautiful woman—then a terrifying eclipse—then a member of the family.

My imagination would run wild, seeing individual stars as part of yet-to-be charted constellations. It was a childish habit of mine to sketch such constellations, connecting the dots on paper, then standing back to determine whether the tracery resembled anything to me.

During the past week, however, there had been a growing dearth of stars on the screen, and my opportunity to make connections became more infrequent. It had gotten to the point where I had begun to just doodle, drawing lines from the dots to nowhere in particular. I apologize for any harm I may have caused future explorers who may attempt to navigate by my charts—but as the universe is endless (so far as I can tell, anyway), these patterns could eventually turn up somewhere; in which case, my ready-made constellations might be put to good use.

I hate to digress any further—especially from myself—but as any writer worth his salt must have as his goal the universal edification of mankind, perhaps a further observation may be tendered here.

The fact is, my scribbles are really no less outlandish than the everyday constellations with which the indulgent reader is already familiar. It is impossible to guess what could have possessed the minds of the poets who went about naming the stars—excepting, of course, that simple genius who christened "Crux" and "Triangulum." All one need do is to look at other star configurations, to see that through no stretch of the imagination can most of these be reconciled with their names. "Ursa Major" and "Ursa Minor," for example, look more like a cuttlefish and a pig, respectively, than a matching set of bears.

In the course of a diligent study, I have examined this problem further. I am convinced that the proper names of the following constellations should be as follows: "Bootes"— the Kite; "Acquila"—the Teepee; "Perseus"— the Peacepipe; "Pegasus"—the Courthouse; "Leo"—the Golf Course; and "Draco"—the Deathmask of Ramses II.

Before taking issue with any of my replacement names, the astronomer and general reader alike must bear in mind that I have seen all these constellations recently, up close.

ii. I spot another movement on the horizon—make camp for the night—an introduction to the Free People—some personal reflections

Instead of moping about, I decided to head for town. I was monarch of all I surveyed, but the time seemed ripe for abdication. The poetaster sun had risen to its most sublime zenith and was waning melodramatically; the cacti refused to do anything but stand at attention; I had seen more activity in empty museum cases. Out of the goodness of my heart, I kept giving the ashen sand its freedom, rubbing it from my eyes and releasing it from my mouth's clamped Bastille.

Imagine my surprise when, about a mile from the ship, I saw several shadowy shapes racing across the horizon. My eyes blinked open—my jaw dropped—I drew in a lot of sand. Then the shapes were gone!

My first inclination was to duck back into the ship immediately. Then I heard an inner voice that was either science or foolhardiness calling me, and I found my courage.

Thereafter, I put my courage away, wiped my lips, and did the only thing a rational creature could do in such a situation: I drew my gun.

A mile or so onwards, and I had just about convinced myself that the long confinement in the ship, combined with the afternoon in a torrid climate, had sautéed my brains.

My exhaustive struggle with the elements was about over, as far as I was concerned—on the one hand, my sojourn on this planet had borne no relationship whatsoever to a romantic adventure tale. On the other hand, I had easily gathered enough material to return to the ship and make one up.

Ahead of me, I saw what appeared to be a few scattered tumbleweeds. One of them rolled in my direction a little. With a start, it occurred to me that these must have been the rolling shapes I had seen before on the horizon—the objects of my long chase.

Well, I'll bet I was disappointed then. To relieve my fury, I pulled out my gun and fired off several shots at one of the tumbleweeds, which burst into flames and vaporized.

I thought it only my imagination when I heard a noise like the one a table makes when dragged across the floor—a wooden screeching.

I decided to take a nap before heading back to the ship. There was a brackish pool of chemicals off to one side, but I did not trust the water qua water. I took a few gulps from my canteen instead. Then I curled up next to a tumbleweed that didn't look like a snorer, and promptly fell asleep.

I must have dozed for hours. My sleep was enhanced by a gentle crackling noise that seemed to emanate from a congenial distance away from me, like a campfire.

My translator was in my breast pocket, and at one time or another during the course of my nap it must have switched on, because gradually the campfire noise began to sound like several whispering voices.

Is it sleeping?

It is restless.

Will it burrrn us?

It is sleeping.

We must kill it!

I looked around me but could see nothing my canteen and the tumbleweed, and since mistrusting my senses had become almost second nature to me on this planet—sort of a way of keeping myself company, you might say—I fell back asleep.

A little later, I had a dream that I was hiking through a forest and the vines were whipping against my arms. Shortly afterwards, the impression of pain seemed to take upon a distinct vivacity, though I still believed the forest was only an idea in my head. Gradually, however, the distinctness of the agony I ventured to say I was feeling, grew acute enough so that I believed I had support for a tenable hypothesis—namely, that the source of my torture was in the external environment! I yelled aloud in my excitement over this important metaphysical discovery.

"Stop! No more!"

I was surrounded—oh yes, I opened my eyes now.   Around me my ring of tumbleweed attackers rolled and bounced away.

I relaxed, considerable. The tallest of them was only knee-high to me, and besides, I still had my gun, which could end the game quickly if I ever got tired of punting them across the terrain.

I pulled it out, now, and began to woo the bushmen with a little advanced technology, firing at a nearby cactus, which sizzled and vaporized.

I now held the floor, and began to address the frightened sagebrush assembly.

"My friends," I said, "fear not. I come in peace, from a planet up space quite a ways. Now, I don't intend to hurt you boys, but I do recall having more pleasant awakenings in the past, and a man can only stand so much. So if you are rational creatures, like myself, I beg you to kindly forbear from such physicality in the future."

Well, I'll bet the bushmen were sorely penitent then, asking me over and over if they had hurt me. They had a peculiar way of talking, always inviting a yes-or-no answer to their questions, but never answering my own, instead rolling away from the subject, true to their contour, and to my great exasperation.

It was only by exercising a good deal of patience (and such exercise does not come naturally to me) that I learned that the tumbleweeds would come around to my question if I plied them with general statements first, such as "You are dry"— to which they might reply, "We have roots"; or, "You seem happy and free"—to which they might bemoan the fact they had no politicians.

Upon learning this trick, I was subsequently able to find out a good deal about their way of life. Their name for themselves is the "Free" (in the sense of "free-moving") people, or the "Rollers." Their lifestyle is a peculiar nomadic one. The Rollers do not eat or photosynthesize; their only nourishment is obtained through groundwater. About once a month or so, for a stretch of six or seven days, they must "put down roots" to refuel. During this interim they cannot readily extricate themselves, for the water table is extraordinarily low, and the taproots sunk into the ashen sand run deep.

Despite their name, the Free people exercise little actual control over their own trajectory. They tire easily of turning more than a few somersaults during a single sally, preferring to blow with the wind when making trips of any substantial distance. Though by the same token, the greatest fear of any Roller is being seized by a mighty sirocco and "blown away" forever.

The Rollers—if the reader considers their spare lifestyle, and the limited say they have in steering themselves toward a destination of their own choosing—are surprisingly selective of company. They often jockey for the same refueling spots and play a spirited game of "poison" trying to bump undesirables off a claim. It is not at all uncommon for a Roller to starve to death by eradication rather than spend an entire week refueling next to one of his unloved brethren.

In fact, I learned that I was somewhat of a hero to the tribe I had just encountered, as the tumbleweed I had shot earlier turned out to be an irrepressible old gaffer who was keen on the filibuster. This proverbial long talker kept all the boys (they numbered twelve or thirteen, if memory serves me correct) writhing and straining at their roots for five solid days with a few tomes of autobiography, plus a travelogue revealing how that part of the country had looked in his younger days, back when a tumbleweed was a tumbleweed.

All major altercations among the Rollers develop out of unfortunate circumstances such as these. I held it as a high mark of their sage ingenuity, that the Rollers have actually invented methods of killing one another other despite their ridiculous shape. Crude is their technology in comparison with ours—and wholly lacking in any advanced weaponry with which to mercifully speed up wars—but I shall refrain here from glorious ethnocentrism.

Roller wars take a great deal of patience, and choreography. I was lucky enough to be witness at one of these contests. It had arisen when five Rollers camped at a prime watering spot held by five members of the opposing party. The two sides lined up, as if for a square dance.

Next, one at a time, a member of each contingent rolled out into the middle of the desert floor, colliding as zestily as possible with the enemy. He would return to the line after that. The governing rule was that whoever sparked first, lost. I do not think it likely that the Rollers were evolved from asbestos.

The Roller war was not designed for the spectator, if I may editorialize for just this once. I began to drowse off as the combatants took turns at each other for hours, trying to get the sparks flying. I did not complain, though. Even if my fingers were aching from having to rewind my wristwatch—and I am not one prone to exaggeration.

Finally, my patience was rewarded—doubly, in fact—when two of the combatants began to spark and smoke at the same time. Then I watched, in great surprise, as they both returned to their sides and set the whole convention on fire!

At this time, I was informed by a companion of mine, who had noticed my astonishment, that such an outcome was not uncommon in a Roller battle. The casual tone in which he disclosed this fact to me alarmed me a little, and diminished my opinion of his species' shrewdness somewhat. *Because what good could a war accomplish, if both sides were annihilated?* I thought to myself. Who would be left holding the real estate?—to claim righteousness?

I shook my head—it was all beyond the understanding of a miserable creature such as myself. To me, the square dances appeared to be nothing but turkeys, and straw.

iii.   I become the talk of the town—some further reflections upon the Rollers—the tale of "Sir Kutus, wandering through the Desert"

The Rollers are exceeding fond of storytelling, and are atrocious liars. I was instantly a celebrity. They would beg me to recite tale after tale and had a predilection for all stories of desert wanderers, from the Crusaders to the Legionnaires, from Moses to Christ to Mohamet. To please them, I made up the story of Sir Kutus, below, of which they were prodigious fond.

At first I thought it my diplomatic duty to teach the Rollers something about myself and the planet I hailed from. After a time, however, I began to notice they seemed not to care, one way or the other, whether I was relating to them the factual truth. Apparently, the Rollers had been spinning such increasingly fantastic yarns to one another to stave off boredom they had long ago lost the faculty of being able to discern the difference.

I confess I had often dreamed of finding such an audience. The Rollers would literally root at my feet for a week or more at a time, during which interval I could get away with just about any piece of rhetorical high coloring ever invented by myself or my fellow authors.

One day I attempted to design a tale specifically for my Roller friends. I lived to regret that day; this tale, which was about a knight named Sir Kutus, was so successful that, from that point forward, the Rollers would hear of no one else but their new hero.

As the reader might be curious to see this tale—and as nothing short of an operation could remove it from my memory, at this point—I present here a partial synopsis.

The Tale of Sir Kutus,
Wandering through the Desert

A strong wind came one day to the place where a young Roller and his family were refueling and blew the child, whose roots were shallow, out from his resting spot. His firmly-rooted father and mother watched, fixated, as the cruel wind carried their son far away. Later, they would search for him far and wide, but they never found the child again.

The orphaning zephyr blew the young Roller to a kingdom at the other side of the world. He bounced over the moat, and bowled and tumbled right up the castle drawbridge into the heart of the childless Queen. This Queen would have adopted the child then and there had the young lad permitted her, but he held out hope that

18

someday he would be reunited with his birth parents. He vowed to set off into the world to find them when he was mature enough.

This day finally came. The Queen shed plentiful tears, begging him to stay, but the Roller felt this pilgrimage was a thing he must do. So the Queen managed a smile then and knighted her little tumbleweed, giving him the name Sir Kutus. She equipped him for his long journey, made him promise to write whenever he could; and sobbing, wished him a good wind. Then he tumbled out of her sight.

Sir Kutus hereupon had many brave adventures . . .

Though he travelled far and wide, he could not discover any word of his lost family. Many years passed; Sir Kutus had long since come of marriageable age. One day he put down roots next to a young female roller of about the same age. She was very beautiful, but jealously protected by her guardian, a distant uncle.

This was a bitter old bramble who had lost his own son years earlier, and the memory of that loss caused him to despise all young Roller men he saw; especially those, like Sir Kutus, who threatened to rob him of his charge. So he forced her to extricate her pretty self from her refueling spot beside her gallant knight . . .

Well, in some accounts, she simply pines away for love (and lack of fuel) and dies; in others, Sir Kutus turns out to be the Old Bramble's son, and succeeds in marrying the fair damsel, but only after wandering through the desert for months first, composing a lot of sickly love sonnets and stabbing them onto cacti. He finally attempts an elopement with the "Burr of his Heart," but her uncle—the old bloodhound—sniffs out their little rendezvous, and lies in ambush for our hero—who is spared at the last moment when the uncle recognizes a birthmark—or spots a scrap of swaddling blanket Sir Kutus wears on his helmet as a token—thereby triggering a memory of the gummy smile of the lost infant (I frequently modified these details for my own amusement). Because, though the plot was simple enough, after a while the Rollers at my feet would hear nothing else; they thought "Sir Kutus" was the greatest thing that had ever tickled their ears; it was their *Iliad*, their *Beowulf*, their *Thousand and One Nights*.

Of course, I modified the ending in all sorts of ways, too, first by making the young damsel just a little more beautiful, and the uncle just a bit more lusty, so that the latter attempts to force her into marriage with himself, only to be thwarted by the honor of Sir Kutus' right arm. That had a nice touch of chivalric romance, but I soon tired of it. So in the scuffle I caused Sir Kutus to kill the irascible old fellow, then later learn he has slain his own father—when he recognizes a scar, or sees something in the gummy leer which recalls the kindly smile of his lost pater. Now I had the stain of Greek tragedy upon my hands! That was depressing, so I

20

changed it up again—this time it was the young *female* roller who turned out to be the lost son in disguise, and I amused myself with a comedy.

I had begun to believe in the arbitrariness of all story endings, when the tale is only a stanchion between someone else's boredom and entertainment. In a final burst of inspiration, I finally made the uncle, in a mad fit, come to believe he was his own son. I wasn't sure what I had then—but it sounded Russian, and I did not doubt it would win me great fame, and a reputation for possessing profound depth of vision.

I'll wager I farmed out every inch of that tale that I could. I began to roll out bale after bale of new characters, planted acres of symbols and other literary embellishments—so that now I had foils to Sir Kutus, antagonists to Sir Kutus, picturesque landscape descriptions, and, for the benefit of the Rollers—or so I thought—long passages of moral instruction.

In truth, the simple tumbleweeds did not always savor the exotic sauces that I poured over the feast of "Sir Kutus." I discovered in them an alarmingly limited vocabulary, and a kind of musical inattention which attached itself to the sounds of words rather than to their meaning.

Unfortunately, I must report that my attempts to civilize the Rollers fell somewhat short of success.

iv.   I draw a vast multitude—a sermon with too much fire, and not enough brimstone.

By this time I was packing in huge crowds. The group I had originally taken up with had just finished refueling, so the members were afterwards able to tag along after me, bouncing with mad abandon like a spilled plate of peas.

My dozen followers increased by hundreds more.   I did my best to entertain them with stories in the afternoons and early evenings. From a technical standpoint, this became more difficult each day—I now had to shout to be heard by the whole assembly.

So when, leading my thistle flock along one day, I came upon a steep precipice rising up from the desert floor, I believed I had found an ideal venue.   Instructing the Roller brethren to wait below, I climbed slowly to the top of the exhausting monadnock.

I paused, wheezed, and panted my way to the top, where I then paused, appropriately, to take in the breathtaking spectacle.   From my new vantage, the round shapes of the Rollers below resembled the heads of a vast human multitude.

The sun poured hot on the ashen sand.   I felt grateful for a partial overhang.   And then I spoke, my voice resonating like Roland's horn.

"My friends, my Roller cousins," I began. "What is your pleasure?"

With a single rasping voice, the crowd demanded its Barabbas; its Sir Kutus. Their drone projected across the desert, scaled the magnificent cliffs, overwhelming me from all sides.

I was impressed, to put it mildly.

But I had decided to first warm up the Rollers with a few anecdotes to put their credulity in the right place for a new ending I had devised to their favorite tale. In it, the old uncle marries the Queen who sponsored and knighted Sir Kutus. They adopt the young female Roller as their daughter. Sir Kutus returns to the kingdom after years of lonely crusading, and his marriage is arranged to the princess. But the knight discovers the new king is his true father, and thus it becomes impossible for him to marry the princess, his royal sister. In a fit of madness, Sir Kutus goes berserk, slaughtering everyone in the castle.

To start off, I told the crowd an anecdote I once heard from an old Yuma Indian. This ancient spoke sadly as he related how a nervous young doctor, newly arrived from the East, had once visited his tribe. The doctor glanced around the village, apparently searching for someone or something, but too embarrassed to ask for directions.

Finally, the green young fellow appeared to spot what he was looking for, walking over to a toothless old Indian mule trader who was grooming one of his animals for the market.

"Can I look at his eyes?" snapped the doctor.

"OK," said the mule trader. So the doctor examined the mule's eyes, but evidently saw something there he didn't like, because as he pulled up each lid, he shook his head and mumbled something under his breath.

"Can I look at his teeth?" he asked next.

"OK," said the mule trader again. So the doctor looked at the teeth, but again saw something he didn't like, because as he pulled up each lip, he shook his head and mumbled again.

"Can you walk him around in a circle?" he asked then.

"OK," the old trader said. "You buy him then?"

"Buy him! Who said anything about buying him?" the doctor retorted. "Why, this is positively the sickest horse I have ever seen!"

I asked the old Yuma what it was about this story that made him so sad to tell it. He answered me that this particular anecdote had spread like wildfire through his village and to the neighboring villages as well. It was soon on the lips of every trader from these villages, translated into dozens of different tribal languages and dialects, and recited across the entire territory. It had spread so quickly that alert cavalry scouts scented a conspiracy, believing the natives were attempting to organize. In self-defense, they ransacked a few central villages, including the old Yuma's.

The Rollers squirmed noticeably; they were always profoundly impatient to hear the latest news of their hero Kutus. But the sound of my own voice carrying was so exhilarating, and the precipice so novel a trumpet to my vanity, that I decided to warm the Rollers further with a few Horace Greeley stories.

I told them the anecdote of Horace Greeley and Hank Monk, which, within a six-year span during which I crossed and re-crossed the Sierras between Nevada and California, I had heard four hundred and eight-two times. Even that one failed to take hold on my audience; the Rollers began to sway in restless anticipation, and to rasp among themselves.

So I decided to limit myself to just one further anecdote in order to prevent an uprising—this final tale, one of my own devising. It had occurred to me a few months back as my ship was leaving the Earth's orbit, and several of the books I had taken along with me had begun to float in solution due to the lack of gravity.

"This made me ponder, my good Roller friends, whether a controlled test might be designed to determine the weightiness of authors in general. Particularly, for those American authors for whom no similar test had been made in the past, as had been done for authors in other countries, by such rigorous scientists as Rabelais, Cervantes, and Swift. Perhaps, I thought, it was because no such trail had as yet been conducted, that the title of 'The Father of American Literature' had yet to be awarded.

"So, for my next voyage, I was careful to take along some literary works of my most famous predecessors and colleagues. I had, among other tomes, one volume each of Irving's and Hawthorne's stories; the collected essays of Emerson; *Walden* by Thoreau; and miscellaneous works by Cooper, Crane, and Whitman.

"All these I placed on a long table which I had set up under the high vault in the central area of the ship. Then I sat down to a hasty breakfast of buckwheat cakes and syrup. The syrup was of my own concoction, a special blend of ingredients gathered from the Mississippi Delta and Southwestern regions of the country. It was 'space food'—I had known it to glue pancakes together with such gravity-defying tenacity that the stack had to be carved from, like ham—and if any dripped onto the plate, the customer would be obliged to eat that, too.

"Also by my side I had placed a large notebook, in which I normally made sketches of my constellations, or jotted notes from my travels. In this book I planned to record my observations.

"Events began to transpire even before I could saw off my first bite of pancake: I heard a hearty hail of volumes against the steel vault of the ship. My surprise was great—and sorrow greater, the reader may rest assured—to find that such a venerable author as Cooper had been the first to meet his fate. His Leatherstocking tales had all bolted for the ceiling with as much team spirit as a chain gang in an escape attempt; though the one about the Mohicans, I noticed, was the last to go.

"I observed one book at the highest point of the ceiling, thumping and putting up the fiercest fight of its life to get out. It was that noblest of savages himself, *Deerslayer*. For fear that he might puncture a hole through the ceiling with his famed marksmanship, I decided to give him his freedom and quickly opened the hatch. When I did, he shot up quicker than Indian corn—and, if he had decided to turn tail then and fall back to Earth a meteorite, I am certain he would have carved out a new ocean.

"If Cooper's poor showing surprised me somewhat, imagine my distress to see Irving go next, who would have been such a neat choice for the Father of our literature: a Washington to match Washington. But we must remember how *familiar* these first writers had to be in order to keep their European correspondents happy—they could not afford to use an ink less light than drollery.

"Crane flew away without much ceremony. Emerson fought a losing battle to keep his tenant, Thoreau; but he himself did not budge at all. An interesting phenomenon occurred with Hawthorne's *Twice-Told Tales*: those pieces containing darker tales of our Puritan ancestors seemed to want to take root in the very table, while some of the lighter tales mutinied from the rest of the book and wrested themselves free. The resulting mass was too slight to hold out much longer.

"This phenomenon stood in direct contrast to the performance made by *Whitman's Leaves of Grass*, which rose as one body, in its entirety, as though making an offering of poems to the heavens. I had not brought with me any Poe, whom I was not sure qualified as an American author at all; and almost sheepishly, I realized I had forgotten to take along any Melville. Certainly I recognized his greatness, his humanity—I had just never purchased any of his books for my own library.

"I experienced such transportations of joy, as cannot easily be described, when I saw that the great Emerson himself was the last of the competitors to remain behind. The great

Concord hymnist lifted his hoary head and riffled his pages as if from a casual nap. Then he rose with dignity and unmatched *gravitas* from the table, hovering few inches above it.

"The experiment was done; I had found my champion of letters—or so it seemed. Because just then I happened to glance over at the other end of the table, and there saw a single page that had slipped out of my memoirs. It had not budged this entire time!

"I blinked my eyes in amazement. I had thought the tone of this piece to be very congenial indeed; it contained, certainly, some of the gentlest and mildest statements of fact I had ever uttered.

"'This cannot be! I told myself.

"I tried blowing on the paper, coaxing it to rise like a snake charmer—still nothing.

"I begged; I blew again; I cajoled. 'Can this mean, then'—I shouted in astonishment—'what it appears? Am I truly more deserving of the prize than all these other worthies'—I gestured wildly in the air—'more deserving than Irving, than Hawthorne, than the mighty Emerson himself?

"I puffed up like a bullfrog with pride—I was in *such* a state of ecstasy! For the moment, I could accomplish nothing further but practice the acceptance speeches for my laureate, and hold the pose I wanted carved on all of my statues.

"While all this time, the page from my memoirs remained motionless on the table.

"My eyes filled with tears of joy—I could hardly regain my composure. But finally, I could no longer resist strutting over to read and commit to memory the single page which had destined me for greatness.

"It was then I noticed that the paper had become discolored around the edges. I examined it more closely, and discovered it had fallen into a puddle of my obstinate pancake syrup!—It could in no way be freed by my efforts to tear it away, and unless I cared to eat the table along with the rest of my breakfast, would remain stuck there forever!

"My friends, that page I wrote remains on my desk still, though it is now a memento of presumption and vanity only."

Well—now I was prepared to joust with Sir Kutus. But it had all been too much for the Rollers. While I spoke, they began squirming uneasily, then bumping and scraping against each other to get to the exits. Sparks began to fly every which way, and before I knew it, the desert floor below me was covered over in a single sheet of fire. . .

THE DIME NOVEL IS MAKING A COMEBACK!

Originating in the late 19th-century and seeing its heyday in the 1940s and 1950s, particularly in genres such as the Western, the format became an important influence on the comic book, the radio drama, and the film and television treatment. Today's "flash novel" is really a new take on an old idea: stories just shy of novelette length, with numbered chapters rather than asterisks, and which, like the movies, compress a narrative otherwise "novelistic" in scope into a short form suitable for a single reading or download.

Red Dashboard LLC is a small indie publishing house seeking intriguing books of poetry and literature: poetry (chapbook and full-length), flash and short story collections, non-fiction, black-and-white artwork.

THE DESERT DIME NOVEL TRILOGY

by M.V. Montgomery (forthcoming in 2014)

BOOK 2

The Double Dare Devil features Skip Eubanks, an old cowboy-turned-stuntman who is paralyzed after a fall from a helicopter. His wife Bonnie now runs the business, but something very sinister is happening to the stuntmen she supplies to the studios.

BOOK 3

Trouble in Paradise Valley tells the story of a big budget Hollywood production that somehow survives star egos, several rewrites, and its own faulty premise. But how long can it last when it intrudes onto a site once sacred to Hohokam skywatchers?